MOHICAN BRAVE

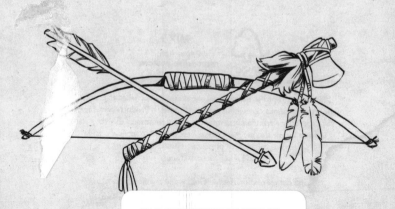

First published in Great Britain by HarperCollins *Children's Books* in 2014
HarperCollins *Children's Books* is a division of HarperCollins *Publishers* Ltd,
77-85 Fulham Palace Road, Hammersmith, London, W6 8JB.

The HarperCollins website address is: www.harpercollins.co.uk

1

Text © Hothouse Fiction 2014
Illustrations © HarperCollins *Children's Books* 2014
Illustrations by Dynamo

ISBN 978-0-00-755002-9

Printed and bound in England by Clays Ltd, St Ives plc

CHRIS BLAKE

TiME HUNTERS

MOHICAN BRAVE

HarperCollins *Children's Books*

Travel through time with Tom
on more

adventures!

For games, competitions and more visit:

www.time-hunters.com

CONTENTS

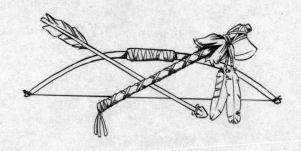

With special thanks to Lisa Fieldler

PROLOGUE

1500 AD, Mexico

As far as Zuma was concerned, there were only two good things about being a human sacrifice. One was the lovely black pendant the tribal elders had given her to wear. The other was the little Chihuahua dog the high priest had just placed next to her.

I've always wanted a pet, thought Zuma, as the trembling pup snuggled up close. *Though this does seem like an extreme way to get one.*

Zuma lay on an altar at the top of the Great Pyramid. In honour of the mighty Aztec rain god, Tlaloc, she'd been painted bright blue and wore a feathered headdress.

The entire village had turned out to watch the slave girl being sacrificed in exchange for plentiful rainfall and a good harvest. She could see her master strutting in the crowd below, proud to have supplied the slave for today's sacrifice. He looked a little relieved too. And Zuma couldn't blame him. As slaves went, she was a troublesome one, always trying to run away. But she couldn't help it – her greatest dream was to be free!

Zuma had spent the entire ten years of her life in slavery, and she was sick of it. She knew she should be honoured to be a sacrifice, but she had a much better plan – to escape!

"Besides," she said, frowning at her painted skin, "blue is not my colour!"

"Hush, slave!" said the high priest, Acalan, his face hidden by a jade mask. "The ceremony is about to begin." He raised his knife in the air.

"Shame I'll be missing it," said Zuma. "Tell Tlaloc I'd like to take a *rain* check." As the priest lowered the knife, she pulled up her

knees and kicked him hard in the stomach
with both feet.

"*Oof!*" The priest doubled over, clutching
his belly. The blade clattered to the floor.

Zuma rolled off the altar, dodging the
other priests, who fell over each other in their
attempts to catch her. One priest jumped into
her path, but the little Chihuahua dog sank
his teeth into the man's ankle. As the priest
howled in pain, Zuma whistled to the dog.

"Nice work, doggie!" she said. "I'm getting

out of here and you're coming with me!" She
scooped him up and dashed down the steps
of the pyramid.

"Grab her!" groaned the high priest from
above.

Many hands reached out to catch the slave
girl, but Zuma was fast and determined.
She bolted towards the jungle bordering
the pyramid. Charging into the cool green
leaves, she ran until she could no longer hear
the shouts of the crowd.

"We did it," she said to the dog. "We're free!"

As she spoke, the sky erupted in a loud rumble of thunder, making the dog yelp. "Thunder's nothing to be scared of," said Zuma.

"Don't be so sure about that!" came a deep voice above her.

Zuma looked up to see a creature with blue skin and long, sharp fangs, like a jaguar. He carried a wooden drum and wore a feathered headdress, just like Zuma's.

She knew at once who it was. "Tlaloc!" she gasped.

The rain god's bulging eyes glared down at her. "You have dishonoured me!" he bellowed. "No sacrifice has ever escaped before!"

"Really? I'm the first?" Zuma beamed

with pride, but the feeling didn't last long. Tlaloc's scowl was too scary. "I'm sorry!" she said quietly. "I just wanted to be free."

"You will *never* be free!" Tlaloc hissed. "Unless you can escape again…"

Tlaloc banged his drum, and thunder rolled through the jungle.

He pounded the drum a second time, and thick black clouds gathered high above the treetops.

"This isn't looking good," Zuma whispered. Holding the dog tightly, she closed her eyes.

On the third deafening drum roll, the jungle floor began to shake and a powerful force tugged at Zuma. She felt her whole body being swallowed up inside… the drum!

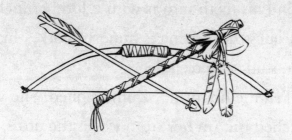

CHAPTER 1
HARVEST TIME

"How many apples do we need to make a crumble?" asked Tom. He was perched on a branch of the apple tree that grew in their back garden.

His mother, who was busy raking brown and gold leaves into a pile, looked in the basket at the base of the tree. "That's plenty!" she said.

"Good. Then this one is mine!" said Tom, picking a ripe apple from the tree and sinking his teeth into it with a loud crunch.

"I guess harvesting is hungry work," his mum said with a smile.

"Tell me about it!" Zuma sighed. She was stretched out on her stomach in the grass, watching Tom pick the fruit. "When I was a slave my master had acres of crops. And guess whose job it was to pick everything? Mine! But I wasn't allowed to eat anything."

Tom's mother couldn't hear Zuma – or see her, either. Nobody except Tom could hear or see Zuma when they weren't on an adventure.

It was still hard for Tom to believe that his friend had lived hundreds of years earlier in ancient Mexico. He had accidentally freed the Aztec slave girl and her feisty dog, Chilli, from their imprisonment in a drum that he'd found in his father's museum. Since then, they had been travelling through time together in search of six golden sun coins that would buy Zuma her freedom. So far they had found four of them.

Zuma reached over to the compost heap and plucked a steak bone from the pile. Chilli sat up on his haunches, panting happily. Zuma tossed him the bone. The Chihuahua caught it in his teeth, chewed it a bit, then began digging a hole to bury it in. Clumps of grass and dirt flew up everywhere. He nearly choked on his apple when Mum's rake brushed dangerously close to Chilli's bottom. She couldn't see the little dog, either.

Mum stopped raking and frowned at the dirt on her otherwise tidy lawn. "Where are all these holes coming from?" she wondered aloud.

"Er, rabbits?" said Tom, gulping down

his last bite of apple with an innocent shrug. "Moles, maybe?"

"Maybe we should call in an exterminator," Mum said.

Chilli stopped digging and let out a nervous yelp.

Tom gave Chilli a stern look. "I'll fill in the holes and I'm sure there won't be any more," he assured his mother.

"Let's hope not," Mum said, wandering back to the house.

Tom picked the biggest apple he could find, then swung down from the tree and tossed it to Zuma with a grin. "Try one of these!" he said.

Zuma bit into the apple and closed her eyes. "Mmmmm," she said, sighing happily. "Eating fruit is a lot more fun than harvesting it. Now that I'm free, I just want to relax."

"*Almost* free," Tom corrected, making his way towards Mum's vegetable patch. "We still have two more coins to find before you can go back to Aztec times."

Zuma finished her apple and tossed the core on to the compost pile.

"Have you ever seen one of these before?" Tom asked, pointing to a pumpkin.

Zuma nodded. "We grew them in my master's garden. The seeds are tasty when they're roasted. Sometimes we'd carve out the shells and use them for containers."

"We make jack-o'-lanterns with them," Tom said, grinning.

"What are they?" said Zuma.

"First you carve out a scary face," said Tom. "Then you put a candle inside, and they glow. We use them as decorations for Halloween. That's the last day in October. It's a special night when kids go from door to door asking for sweets!"

"In Aztec times we called that begging,"

said Zuma.

"This is different," Tom explained. "It's called trick-or-treating. Part of the fun is that we get dressed up in silly, scary costumes." Zuma looked at her blue painted skin, feathery headdress and distinctive black stone pendant. "I bet nobody has a costume as good as mine."

Tom laughed. "Yes, you'd have the best Halloween costume ever."

"I can think of an even better costume," said Zuma. "You could go trick-or-treating as someone *really* scary – Tlaloc!" Zuma picked up Mum's rake and thumped the handle against the pumpkin like it was a drum. "I am the god of thunder!" she boomed in a deep voice. "I'm a great big bully who sacrifices little kids!"

Tom and Zuma burst out laughing. But

their laughter was suddenly drowned out by the sound of thunder rumbling through the sky. Suddenly the Aztec god appeared in front of them. His eyes were practically goggling out of his blue face in rage.

"How dare you mock me, slave girl!" Tlaloc bellowed, stomping his enormous feet and scattering leaves all over the grass. "You forget that you have not purchased your freedom yet!" He crossed the garden, squashing flowers and vegetables as he went. "You must find two more coins first." He bared his sharp fangs as he let out a nasty chuckle. "Though I doubt you will be brave enough to succeed!"

A shining mist swirled up from the ground. Zuma dropped the rake and grabbed Tom's hand. The wind howled, spinning the mist faster and faster around them.

"Here we go!" said Tom.

"Chilli!" cried Zuma.

The little dog leaped into her arms just as Tlaloc's magic whisked them into the hazy darkness of space and time.

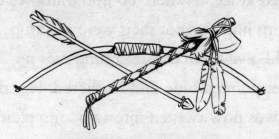

CHAPTER 2
DEER HUNTER

They landed with a bump in a wood. When the mist cleared, the autumn air was fresh and crisp, with a pleasant earthy smell. Tom looked around and saw that the trees blazed with colour. The leaves were different shades of red, orange and gold. The undergrowth was thick with green ferns, and in the distance Tom caught sight of a sparkling blue river.

"Wow! It's so pretty," Zuma said in a

hushed voice. "Where do you think we are?"

Tom hoped what they were wearing would give them a clue. Zuma was no longer painted blue and feathered. Her dark hair was now twisted into two long plaits. The black necklace was the only thing that

remained of her Aztec clothing. Both she and
Tom were dressed in soft leather breeches
and tunic-style shirts. Leather fringes
dangled from their sleeves and the front was
decorated with beaded patterns. On their
feet they wore beaded leather moccasins.
Tom had seen similar ones in the North
American section at his father's museum.

"We're dressed like Native Americans,"
he said. "But North America is a really big
continent so I'm not sure exactly where we
are."

Zuma hugged her arms round her and
shivered. "Brr!" she said. "It's certainly
colder than where I come from. The sooner
we find that coin the better!"

"Then let's see what your pendant has to
say," Tom suggested.

Zuma took the black disc in her hand and

held it up to the light to recite the familiar
incantation:

> *"Mirror, mirror, on a chain.*
> *Can you help us? Please explain!*
> *We are lost and must be told*
> *How to find the coins of gold."*

There was a shimmer of silver across the
gleaming stone as words rose to the surface:

> *On the banks of the water*
> *You'll find a sun, then seek a daughter;*
> *With the bravest of braves you'll use your wiles*
> *To find the pretty stream that smiles.*
> *Weather's mysteries you shall know:*
> *You'll shiver with your quiver in an early snow,*
> *But October storms are soon to melt.*
> *The treasure lies within a belt.*

Zuma sighed. "Why can't it ever just say, 'the coin is hidden under the third tree on the right'?"

Tom was about to reply that it wouldn't be much of a riddle if it did, but before he could open his mouth, Chilli caught the scent of something. The dog let out an excited bark and dashed deeper into the woods.

"Let's go!" cried Zuma, taking off after him.

Tom followed, kicking up dried leaves as he ran. Chilli was in hot pursuit of a small brown and white rabbit. The rabbit disappeared down a hole and Chilli would have followed if Zuma hadn't reached out and caught him.

"Where are you going, silly?" she asked. "We need you to help us find the coin."

As he tried to catch his breath, Tom

caught a glimpse of gold glittering between some bushes. *Could it be the coin?* he wondered. Tlaloc never usually made their tasks so easy. He grabbed Zuma's sleeve and pointed.

Then from within the undergrowth, a creature stepped forward, two shining gold eyes staring out from its face.

"Hello, little doggie!" cried Zuma in delight.

Chilli began to wag his tail and wriggle in Zuma's arms.

"Chilli wants to make friends," said Zuma.

The creature swished its bushy orange tail. Zuma was about to set Chilli back down on the ground, but Tom stopped her just in time.

"That's not a dog," Tom said. "It's a fox." He patted Chilli on the head. "Better keep your distance, boy. Foxes can be dangerous. Their teeth and claws are very sharp."

Chilli let out a whimper of disappointment and they carried on exploring the forest. Aside from the rustling of leaves and the chirping of birds, the woods were silent. There didn't seem to be any paths, and there was no sign of a town or city anywhere.

"I wonder if we're the only people here," Tom said aloud.

An odd warbling noise suddenly echoed through the woods. Moments later, a flock of birds trotted into view. Dark feathers fanned out from their backs, and lumpy red skin dangled from their necks.

Zuma hid behind Tom and shuddered. "Ugh!" she said. "Are those hideous creatures dangerous too?"

Tom laughed. "No," he said. "Turkeys

won't hurt you, they just look strange."

"I think you mean *ugly*," said Zuma. Suddenly, her eyes went wide and she pointed. "Duck!" she cried, pulling on his arm.

"Not duck, *turkey*," Tom corrected her.

"No... *duck*!" Zuma dropped to the ground, just as an arrow came whizzing over her head.

Too late, Tom understood what she was

saying. He whirled round in the direction the arrow had come from and saw a flash of feathers sticking out from behind a tree. Then he heard a *thwang* and a *whoosh*...

Another arrow flew through the air and tore through his shoulder.

"Owwwww!" Tom howled in pain.

He looked at his arm. The sleeve of his buckskin shirt had torn and blood was trickling out of a gash.

"Tom!" cried Zuma, pulling him to the ground. "Are you OK?"

Tom nodded and tried not to let out another moan. "I don't think it's too deep," he said through gritted teeth.

"I guess that answers your question," Zuma said, as another arrow whizzed past them. They caught a flash of bright feathers sticking out from behind a tree trunk.

"What do you mean?" Tom asked.

"We definitely aren't the only people around!" Zuma said. "And whoever else is here doesn't seem very happy about having company!"

A dark-haired figure dressed in buckskins stepped out from behind the tree, his bow poised, an arrow already held against the taut string.

And it was pointed directly at Tom's heart.

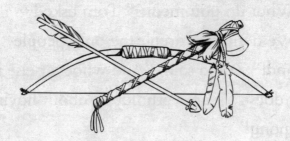

CHAPTER 3

RISING SUN

"Please don't shoot!" said Tom, hoping
that the stranger would understand him.
That's how Tlaloc's magic had always
worked in the past. But with an arrow
aimed straight at his chest, he couldn't take
anything for granted. Tom put his hands
in the air to show the stranger he meant
no harm.

As the stranger came closer, Tom could
see that he was only a boy, not much older

than they were. He wore brilliantly beaded
buckskins and his cheeks were smeared
with swirls of yellow and red paint. Like
Zuma, his long hair had
been wound into two
glossy plaits. Around
his forehead was a
beaded band with
two bright crimson
feathers sticking
out of it.

"I like your paint and feathers," Zuma remarked in her friendliest voice. "Have you ever thought of trying a bit of blue? It's not a bad look."

The boy blinked at her, confused.

"It's probably not the time to give him fashion advice," Tom whispered, "when he's got an arrow pointed at my chest."

As if remembering what he was doing, the boy quickly lowered the weapon. Tom heaved a sigh of relief.

"I'm so sorry!" said the boy. "I didn't mean to hurt you. I thought you were a deer." He gave them an embarrassed grin. "Actually, I *hoped* you were."

"Don't worry," said Tom, clutching his wounded arm. "Accidents happen."

The boy bent down to examine Tom's wound. "It's not too bad," he said. "But it's still bleeding." He crouched beside the roots of a tall tree and gathered up a handful of green moss.

"This is no time for gardening," huffed Zuma.

The boy laughed. "This isn't gardening, it's medicine." A dark look passed over his face as something had just occurred to him. "You're not Mohawk, are you?"

"I'm an Aztec," said Zuma.

"And I'm British," said Tom.

The boy thought it over, then shrugged. "I do not know either of those tribes. But as long as you're not Mohawk, I am happy to help you."

Tom watched as the boy pressed the clump of fuzzy green moss to his cut. In seconds, the moss soaked up the blood.

"That's clever," said Tom.

"Yes," said the boy, crossing to a young willow tree and peeling off some strips of bark. "And this willow bark will make a good healing tonic once I take it home and boil it up. Do you feel well enough to walk to my village? It's not far, just round the bend there."

"Village?" said Zuma, sounding relieved. "So there are other people here?"

The boy nodded and helped Tom to his feet. "Yes. My people are called the Mohican." He started walking towards the water. Tom and Zuma followed.

"My name is Rising Sun," the boy said. "What are you called?"

Tom replied for both of them. "I'm Tom, and this is Zuma."

Chilli let out an indignant bark.

"And this is Chilli," added Zuma, giving the dog a pat.

As they travelled through the woods, Tom noticed how silently Rising Sun moved, avoiding things like fallen twigs. Tom copied him, trying to walk as quietly as he could.

"We call ourselves Mohican," Rising Sun explained, "because it means 'People of the waters that are never still'."

Tom eyed the swift current churning under the surface of the wide blue river. It sparkled in the autumn sunlight. "I can see why," he said.

"Why were you worried that we might be members of the Mohawk tribe?" Zuma asked.

Rising Sun scowled. "Because they are enemies of the Mohicans. They live on the other side of the river. And they are trying to drive us away so they can have these hunting grounds for themselves."

"That doesn't sound very fair," said Zuma.

"Is that why you're wearing war paint?" Tom asked excitedly. "Because you're going into battle with the Mohawk?"

Rising Sun touched the squiggles he'd painted on his cheeks and forehead. "We believe these symbols and colours have magical powers." He smiled sheepishly. "And I need all the help I can get."

"What do you mean?" asked Tom.

"I'm a terrible hunter," the boy admitted, looking embarrassed. He nodded towards Tom's shoulder. "I mistook you for a deer."

Zuma gave a wave of her hand. "It could happen to anyone."

"That's the problem," sighed Rising Sun. "I'm not just anyone. I'm the son of Chief Tall Oak. My father is our tribe's leader and also our greatest hunter and warrior. So of course I'm expected to be like him."

"Maybe all you need is a little practice," Tom suggested.

"But I don't want to be either of those things," Rising Sun explained. "What I really want is to be a medicine man. I like caring for others, and I'm good at healing injuries."

"My, er, *tribe* calls that being a doctor," said Tom. "And doctors are very important and highly respected."

"Why can't you just tell your dad you'd rather be a medicine man?" asked Zuma.

Rising Sun shook his head sadly. "The son of a powerful chief is expected to be a brave warrior. That's why I was sent out here alone today – to test my hunting skills and prove my bravery. But as you can see, I haven't done very well. I'm going home empty-handed."

"No, you're not," said Zuma, scooping Chilli into her arms. "You've got us! And we're much more interesting than a smelly old deer!" She giggled, but her joke failed to cheer up Rising Sun.

"My father won't be proud of me," the boy said darkly. "A hunter has to feed his family, and a warrior must be able to fight skilfully. I can't do either." He pointed ahead to a cluster of small, round huts. "Here is my village."

"Great!" said Zuma. "I'm freezing. Do you think there'll be a fire where I can warm up?"

"Of course," said Rising Sun. "My people are very friendly and welcoming."

The words were no sooner out of his mouth when Tom heard Zuma gasp. Three huge Mohican braves stepped soundlessly into their path, blocking their way.

Tom turned to go back the way they had come, but found himself staring up at three more Mohican braves who had appeared silently behind them. These warriors were as frightening as the first three. All six wore feathered headbands and held sharp weapons, poised to strike.

Tom looked up into their painted faces and tried to remember what Rising Sun had said about his tribe being friendly and welcoming. Because as the braves glared down at him, Tom wasn't feeling very welcome at all!

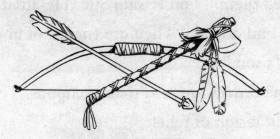

CHAPTER 4
WIGWAM WELCOME

"Drop your weapons!" said Rising Sun.

Nobody moved. Tom gulped, sizing up the band of warriors who blocked their path. They all held tomahawks that looked like they could cut through him like butter.

"Let us past," ordered Rising Sun.

The strongest-looking brave narrowed his eyes. "Not until you tell us who these strangers are."

"They were lost in the woods, and I

helped them," said Rising Sun. He lifted his chin and added, "They are friends of your chief's son."

The braves lowered their weapons. Tom let out a sigh of relief.

"We are sorry to have stopped you, Rising Sun," said the strongest brave. "We were scouting for Mohawk in the area. They have become bolder these last few weeks."

Rising Sun nodded. "You were right to stop us, Gliding Eagle."

"How did your hunting mission go?" asked another brave, his eyes twinkling mischievously. "I see you are returning without so much as a chipmunk."

Rising Sun lowered his eyes.

"Leave him alone, Waning Moon," said Gliding Eagle. "I'm sure Rising Sun would have shot something if he hadn't stopped to help these strangers." With a polite nod to Rising Sun, he stepped out of the way and the three children continued on towards the village.

The Mohican settlement of round-topped

wigwams wasn't enclosed by any sort of wall or fence. It was completely unprotected.

No wonder they're so worried about an attack, thought Tom.

The whole village was bustling with

activity. Children played with corn dolls and practised shooting with toy bows and arrows. The women were busy cooking, some of them carrying babies on their backs.

"We are preparing for the cold winter

ahead," Rising Sun explained. He cast a grim glance towards a group of braves who were sharpening spears and axes. "And because of the Mohawk threat, our weapons must always be ready."

A shiver ran down Tom's spine. He and Zuma exchanged worried looks. They followed Rising Sun to the centre of the village, where a group of older men sat cross-legged round a fire.

"That's my father," said Rising Sun, motioning to a stern-looking man. "Chief Tall Oak."

The chief was as solidly built as the trunk of a tree. His stern face was covered in tattoos, and like the other men he wore a beaded band round his forehead, with a single feather jutting out of it. His hair had been closely shaved on the sides, leaving a single strip down the middle from his crown to the nape of his neck.

"You have brought no deer," said Tall Oak in a deep voice.

"I'm sorry, Father," murmured Rising Sun.

The chief took a long suck on the carved wooden pipe he was smoking. His eyes never left his son as he unfolded his long legs and stood. His height was as impressive as his name suggested.

"What will we eat tonight, without meat? How will our braves remain strong to fight the Mohawk?" Now Tall Oak's black eyes flicked over the strangers hovering nearby. "That little dog would not feed even a small child."

Chilli whimpered in fear and buried his head in Zuma's shoulder.

"I'm sorry," said Rising Sun again. "But I was trying to—"

"Shoot the biggest deer you've ever seen!" Tom interrupted.

"Right," Zuma added, playing along. "It was charging out of the trees, right towards us. Rising Sun had his bow aimed and his arrow ready—"

"But I panicked," said Tom, "and I ran right between Rising Sun and the deer. That's how I got hurt." Tom didn't like lying to this important man, but Rising Sun had been so kind to them, it was now their turn to help him.

Chief Tall Oak looked at his son for a long, quiet moment.

"That's not true," Rising Sun admitted, stepping forward. "My new friends are trying to spare me the shame of what really happened." He let out a heavy sigh. "I thought Tom was a deer and I shot him." Again, the chief was silent. He lifted his pipe to his lips and puffed, then exhaled a cloud of smoke. Tom wished he could tell what the tall man was thinking.

"May I take Tom to the medicine man now?" Rising Sun asked softly.

The chief nodded and went back to the fire. Tom and Zuma followed Rising Sun across the village to a long, narrow bark-covered dwelling.

"This is Wise Owl's longhouse," said Rising Sun in a respectful tone. "He is our healer and spiritual leader."

Inside the longhouse, a smouldering fire sent up clouds of fragrant smoke. As Tom's eyes adjusted to the gloom, he could just make out the shape of a very old man with long silver hair and a deeply lined face. His eyes were closed, but his lips moved slightly as he whispered a string of strange words.

"He's chanting," Rising Sun explained. "Talking to the spirits and asking for their guidance. He's in a trance so we must wait." Rising Sun busied himself with tearing the bark he'd collected into smaller pieces.

"Let's have a look around – the coin might be somewhere in here," Tom whispered to Zuma.

Trying not to make it too obvious, Tom and Zuma searched the medicine man's longhouse. The floor was strewn with animal skins and woven blankets. There were lots of dried herbs bunched together, as well as several hollowed-out gourds. But there was no sign of the gold coin.

At last, Wise Owl stopped chanting and

walked slowly towards them. Rising Sun explained to the medicine man what had happened in the woods.

Wise Owl examined the wound on Tom's arm and nodded approvingly. He put a leathery hand on Rising Sun's shoulder. "A good medicine man understands that nature will always provide. You used your instincts well and helped a friend."

Rising Sun seemed to glow under the medicine man's praise. Together, the two of them brewed a tonic with the willow bark. As they waited for it to boil, Wise Owl began to chant again.

"He's asking the spirits to help heal your wound," Rising Sun told Tom.

"For your sake," Zuma whispered, pulling a face and fanning the air beneath her nose, "I hope he's asking them to make that stuff taste better than it smells too."

When the brew was ready, Wise Owl poured the steaming liquid into a hollow gourd.

Tom drank it. It tasted horrible, but as the warmth of the drink spread through him, he realised that the pain in his arm was vanishing.

"Wow," he said. "That stuff really works."

"It always does," said Wise Owl, smiling. He reached down to give Chilli, who was curled up on a raccoon fur, a friendly pat on the head. "I called upon the great energy of your animal guide to aid my prayers."

Chilli yelped as though to say, "Who, me?"

Tom raised an eyebrow. "You're joking?"

Wise Owl chuckled. "This little dog has a big spirit."

Outside the longhouse, a few people were building a new wigwam. They were bending young trees into a rounded frame. Tom and Zuma helped by holding branches in place while Rising Sun tied them together tightly. Even Chilli got involved, dragging branches over for them to use. When the frame was built, they covered it with sheets of tree bark.

With so many helpers, the snug little house was soon finished.

"Wow!" said Tom, impressed. "It takes my tribe months to build a house."

While Rising Sun helped a family move into the new wigwam, Tom and Zuma explored the rest of the village. Just beyond the houses was a field of tall green stalks that bobbed in neat rows as far as the eye could see. As he gazed across the field, Tom caught a glimpse of gold sparkling in the sun. "Zuma," he whispered. "Is that what I think it is?"

Zuma squinted in the direction he was pointing. "I hope so!"

Tom and Zuma ran towards the gold, with Chilli sprinting along behind them. They skidded to a halt by a pretty young girl who was burying something in the ground.

"What's that?" Tom asked breathlessly.

The girl blinked her large dark eyes. "Corn, of course."

The golden sparkle that they'd seen had just been sunlight reflecting off a pile of yellow corn kernels. Zuma let out a frustrated sigh.

"What's wrong?" asked the girl. "Don't you like corn?"

"I love it," said Zuma. "But why are you burying it?"

"To eat during the long winter months," the girl explained, finishing her task and standing up. "Corn doesn't grow in winter. And the weather is beginning to change."

By now, Rising Sun had caught up with them. "I see you've met my sister," he said. "Laughing Brook, these are my new friends, Tom and Zuma. And Chilli."

Laughing Brook, thought Tom. What had the riddle said? 'A stream that smiles.' Maybe Rising Sun's sister would lead them to the coin!

"I am happy to meet you," said Laughing Brook. She patted Chilli and gave him a little treat from her pocket. Chilli gobbled it up and begged for more.

"I guess Chilli likes deer jerky," said Laughing Brook. "Speaking of deer…" she gave her brother a concerned look. "How did the hunt go?"

"Not very well," admitted Rising Sun. "I didn't catch anything."

"Don't worry," said Laughing Brook, giving his shoulder a squeeze. "There will be plenty to eat. I'll make corn bread and roasted pumpkin."

"Sounds delicious." Her brother gave her a

knowing grin. "What's the catch?"

"*You* have to help me pick the pumpkins."

Before Rising Sun could complain, they heard a commotion at the centre of the village. Rushing back, they found the braves had joined Chief Tall Oak round the fire. They were all carrying sharp-looking spears that glinted in the sunlight.

"What's going on?" asked Zuma. "Have the Mohawks attacked?"

"No," said Rising Sun with a grin. "It's time to go fishing!"

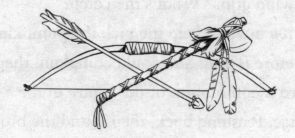

CHAPTER 5
GONE FISHIN'

Zuma ran excitedly over to where the braves were gathered. Tom, Chilli and Rising Sun trailed after her.

"Do you have a spear for me?" she asked the chief.

Tall Oak scowled. "The squaw should remain in the village."

"That's ridiculous!" snapped Zuma. She folded her arms across her chest and shook her head. "I'm brilliant at fishing!"

"Er, our tribe does things a bit differently," Tom explained nervously.

To Tom's surprise, Tall Oak handed Zuma a spear. They followed the braves to the riverbank, where they began dragging canoes over to the water. The boats were made from long logs that had been hollowed out.

Tom and Zuma climbed into Rising Sun's canoe, while Chief Tall Oak, Gliding Eagle and Waning Moon got into another boat.

"Remember the last time we were in a canoe?" Zuma whispered to Tom.

"How could I forget?" Tom replied.

On their last adventure, Tom and Zuma had found themselves in the Stone Age, where they'd narrowly escaped disaster on rushing rapids.

"At least this time we know how to

paddle," Tom said.

Zuma looked at the river's swift current and grinned. "It should be a nice, easy trip."

Tom looked in the bottom of the canoe for bait and fishing lines, but all he saw was some rope. "Where's the fishing tackle?" he asked Rising Sun.

"This is all you need," said Rising Sun, holding up a wooden spear. Rising Sun tied a length of rope to the end of the spear, then attached the other end of the rope to the canoe.

"Why are you doing that?" Tom asked.

"So I can throw my spear further," Rising Sun explained. "It turns it into a harpoon." He grinned at Tom. "And if it falls into the water, I don't have to jump in to get it back!"

Zuma dipped her hand in the water and

shivered. "Good idea," she said, then turned her own spear into a harpoon using another length of rope.

As they pushed off from the bank, Tom dipped his paddle into the water. Zuma sat back and turned her face up to the sun.

"Go ahead – make yourself comfortable," Tom said, rolling his eyes.

"I will," Zuma replied. "You two can paddle. I'm going to relax. Slaves never get to do that, so I'm making up for lost time!"

"But I thought you wanted to fish," said Rising Sun.

"I do," said Zuma. "Wake me up when you see a fish!" She closed her eyes and stretched out her legs. Chilli curled up next to her and began to snore.

As they followed the other canoe, Tom gazed at the trees lining both sides of the river.

Their bright leaves glowed with autumn colours.

"It must be wonderful to live in such a beautiful place," he said to Rising Sun.

"We Mohicans belong here by the river. That's why we won't let the Mohawk tribe drive us away."

The canoe moved swiftly through

the water. Tom suddenly felt as though
someone, or something, was watching them.
He turned his head towards the bank and
thought he saw a flicker of motion through
the leaves.

"Did you see that?" he asked. "That
movement on the shore?"

"I was looking for fish," said Rising Sun,

his spear raised above his shoulder. "It was probably just a deer – they come to the river to drink." He pointed in the distance, at a wood and stone structure built across the river. "We're almost at the weir," he announced.

"The where?" asked Tom.

"Yes, the weir," replied Rising Sun.

Tom looked confused, so Rising Sun explained. "A weir is a pen for catching fish. It keeps them from swimming away, which makes spearing them a lot easier."

As they got closer, Tom could see lots of fish wriggling just below the water's surface. Rising Sun plunged his spear into the river and pulled it back with a fish skewered on the point.

"Brilliant!" cried Tom. Copying his friend's technique, he jabbed his spear into the river.

Unfortunately, he missed.

He missed on the second and third attempts too.

At the sound of Tom's frustrated sigh, Zuma opened one eye. "Problem?"

"I can't seem to get the hang of this," he said.

"Let me try." Zuma took Tom's spear, then she jerked her arm and sent the blade plunging into the weir. To Tom's surprise, she caught a plump, shimmering fish on her very first try.

"Wow!" said Tom, impressed.

Zuma shrugged modestly. "I lived near a lake. My master made me catch fish for his family to eat."

Zuma and Rising Sun caught one fish after another. Before long there was a large heap of silvery fish flopping about at the bottom of the canoe.

Chief Tall Oak called to them from the other canoe. "It's time to head back to the village. There will be plenty of fish for supper!"

Tom and Rising Sun started paddling back the way they had come.

Suddenly, Chilli barked and leaned over the side of the canoe.

"What is it, boy?" Zuma asked.

Chilli wagged his tail and barked at something shimmering just below the water's surface.

"There!" Tom cried, pointing into the water. "A huge fish!"

No sooner had he spoken than the enormous creature sprang out of the river. It flew through the air in a flash of silver before diving back into the water with a loud splash.

"It must be over two metres long!" gasped Tom as he watched it swim away.

"It's a sturgeon!" said Rising Sun.

"Don't let it go!" cried Zuma, reaching for her spear.

Tom and Rising Sun began to paddle at full speed, trying to keep up with the giant fish. Soon they were close enough to make out the diamond-shaped markings along its side.

Zuma quickly threw her spear. It flew through the air, the rope unfurling behind it. The weapon plunged into the water, spearing the enormous fish with its sharp tip.

"You got him!" cheered Tom.

He felt the canoe buck under him.

"Actually," gulped Zuma, "I think *he's* got *us*."

The sturgeon broke the surface of the

water, the spear sticking out of its back. The rope connecting the spear to the canoe pulled taut as the angry fish dived back into the water.

"Here we go!" Rising Sun shouted. "Hold on tightly!"

The huge fish powered through the water, pulling the canoe along with it. It began to swim faster and faster, desperately trying to get free.

Tom and Zuma clung to the side of the canoe as it bounced along. Cold water splashed Tom's face as the sturgeon thrashed about in the water. Suddenly, the fish changed course and the whole boat tilted, nearly tipping them overboard.

"Cut the rope!" shouted Tall Oak.

The chief and the other braves were paddling their canoe as fast as they could, but they couldn't catch up with the frantic fish.

But Rising Sun made no move to cut the rope. "No way!" he said. "I'm not letting it get away."

The sturgeon dived deep, then rose out of the water again. But this time its leap was short and shallow. The fish was getting tired – and so was Tom. He felt as if his arms would break as he desperately held on to the canoe.

The sturgeon summoned one last surge of strength, darted forward and lifted the front of the canoe out of the water. Zuma toppled backwards, landing in Tom's lap. But Rising Sun never lost control, even as the boat slammed down with a splash.

At last, the fish slowed and its fins stopped thrashing. Finally, it stopped moving at all. Tom breathed a sigh of relief as everything was calm once more. He and Rising Sun paddled back to shore and pulled the canoe up on to the bank.

Moments later, the other braves joined them. Tom and Zuma helped Rising Sun haul the gigantic fish out of the water.

Tom expected Rising Sun to show off his big catch, but instead the brave knelt beside the fish. He closed his eyes, raised his hands to the sky and began to murmur softly.

"What's he doing?" Zuma whispered.

"He's giving a blessing," Gliding Eagle explained.

"For a fish?" asked Zuma.

"Yes," said Gliding Eagle. "We believe all life forms are precious, so he is thanking this fish for giving up its life." The warrior closed his eyes and made his own blessing.

When the blessing was complete, Gliding Eagle and Waning Moon helped Rising Sun carry the fish back to the village. Everyone was in good spirits, looking forward to the feast.

"Rising Sun, you showed great bravery," Tall Oak said, placing a large hand on his son's shoulder.

Rising Sun beamed with pride. "Thank you, Father."

But the cheerful mood did not last long. They were halfway to the village when Wise Owl came hobbling down the path towards them, his wrinkled face full of worry.

"Hurry!" the medicine man cried. "The Mohawk have attacked!"

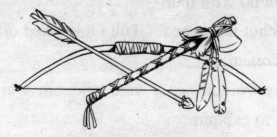

CHAPTER 6
WAR DANCE

Everyone ran back to the village as fast as they could. Tom, Zuma and the elderly medicine man struggled to keep up with Chief Tall Oak and the braves as they raced down the path.

Before they even got to the village, they could hear wails of despair in the distance. When they arrived, they found the entire tribe huddled round the fire. Women were weeping. Children clung to their mothers, trembling with fear.

"What happened?" Tall Oak asked one of the women.

The woman's eyes were wild. She was too upset to explain.

Wise Owl stepped forward, his voice choked with emotion. "The Mohawk attacked while the village was unguarded."

Tom felt a sinking feeling in his stomach. The movement he'd seen on the riverbank must have been Mohawk scouts. When they'd seen that the Mohican warriors were out fishing, they'd known it was the perfect time to attack the camp.

"Has anyone been harmed?" asked Chief Tall Oak.

Wise Owl swallowed hard, then answered, "They have kidnapped Laughing Brook."

The colour drained from the chief's face.

"They have taken my daughter?"

"No!" cried Rising Sun, clenching his fists. "I don't believe it. My sister's too smart to have been caught. She must be hiding!" Tears sprang to his eyes. "Did you look for her?"

The old medicine man confirmed this with a solemn nod.

"Then I will rescue her!" Rising Sun said through gritted teeth. "I'll bring her back."

"And we will help you," Tom promised.

Zuma threw her arms round Rising Sun and hugged him as hard as she could. But Tom could see that Rising Sun didn't want to be comforted. His sister was gone, and was possibly in great danger. The Mohican brave went into a nearby wigwam and came out holding a razor-sharp tomahawk.

It was time to prepare for war!

★

A full moon had risen, and stars shone brightly in the clear black sky. Tom and Zuma sat beside a blazing fire and watched with wide eyes as the braves danced to the pounding of drums. Their blood-curdling whoops and shrieks rang out into the night.

"What are they doing?" Zuma asked, pulling a woven blanket round her shoulders. There was a real chill in the air,

and even Tom felt cold now.

"It's a war dance," Rising Sun panted, as he rested for a moment beside them. "It's how we prepare for battle. We're asking the spirits to guide us to victory."

"I like the music," said Zuma, nodding along to the beat of the drums.

Gliding Eagle, who led the dance, looked terrifying as he stomped around the roaring fire. His face was streaked with war paint, and his tomahawk glinted in the flickering light.

Rising Sun stood to join in the dance again. Tom knew his friend wanted to be a medicine man, not a warrior. But now Laughing Brook was in danger Rising Sun looked just as fierce as the other braves dancing around the fire. He shouted and chanted as he waved his tomahawk menacingly.

"I hope Rising Sun is OK," Tom whispered. "The Mohawks are known for their bloodthirsty instincts."

"Well, the Mohicans look pretty deadly to

me," Zuma whispered back. "They're even scarier than Tlaloc!"

Tom watched as the dance gained momentum, his heart thumping with nervousness and excitement. His feet couldn't resist tapping along to the drums. They seemed to be pounding louder and louder now! In fact, they were as loud as... *thunder*!

The ground shook as Tlaloc stood in front of the fire, feathered and frowning. "So you still have not learned to speak my name with respect," he growled.

"You heard *that*?" Zuma gulped. "Wow, you don't miss a thing, do you!"

"She didn't mean you aren't scary," Tom said quickly. "You're extremely scary."

"I will show you just how terrifying I can be!" Tlaloc boomed, his voice rolling like thunder across the black sky.

Glaring at Zuma with bulging eyes, he lifted his arms above his head and inhaled deeply, filling his lungs with the frosty night air. Then he exhaled a powerful gust of wind. The blast was so icy that a few of the braves stopped dancing to rub their arms. The women and children who were sitting round the fire shivered and pulled their blankets more tightly. With another roll of thunder, Tlaloc vanished.

"What has he done this time?" Zuma asked, her teeth chattering.

"He's made the temperature drop," Tom said. He looked up at the sky, where the glowing moon was now lost behind thick clouds.

Rising Sun approached them. "It's time to go into battle," he said. "It will be very dangerous. You are welcome to join us, but I will understand if you wish to remain here."

Zuma shrugged off her blanket and stood up. "Just try and stop us!"

Tom, Zuma and Chilli followed Rising Sun and the others to the water's edge. Tom's toes felt frozen in his leather moccasins and the wind off the river was so cold his eyes began to water. They got into the canoes and started paddling, but this time they weren't going on a jolly fishing trip – this time they were going to war.

And then he saw them – snowflakes.

Normally Tom would be excited at seeing snow, but this time he realised it would make their mission to save Laughing Brook even harder. He suddenly remembered the words of the riddle: *You'll shiver with your quiver in an early snow.*

"What in the world…?" breathed Zuma.

"Snow," said Tom.

Zuma looked puzzled and Tom realised why – she had never seen snow in ancient Mexico, where it was always hot.

"Basically, it's frozen rain," he explained.

"How strange," said Rising Sun, frowning as more flakes began to spiral out of the sky. "It is very early for snow. Autumn snow is not unheard of, but the sky was clear until a moment ago."

It was clear until Zuma annoyed an Aztec god with magical weather powers, thought Tom grimly.

"We've been expecting a hard winter," Rising Sun went on. "We've seen the signs in the changing of the leaves and in the thickness of the animals' coats." He flicked a few snowflakes off his painted face. "But we did not expect snow to come before the leaves fell from the trees."

The river became slushy as a coating of ice began to form on the water's surface. The storm had become a blizzard by the time they reached the far bank. Ducking into the wind, they hid their canoes behind some bushes, in case any Mohawk scouts were about.

"We don't want to give them any warning," Gliding Eagle explained. "We want to have the element of surprise on our side."

Tom looked down at the ground, now covered by several centimetres of fresh powder. "What about our footprints?" he asked nervously.

Gliding Eagle shook his head. "The fringe on our leggings and moccasins will wipe away our tracks."

"Cool!" said Zuma, shaking her leg to make the fringe swish.

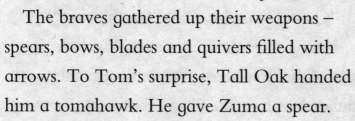

Then Gliding Eagle handed out thick fur cloaks to protect against the freezing air and gusting wind. "These will keep us warm, and help to camouflage us," he said.

The braves gathered up their weapons — spears, bows, blades and quivers filled with arrows. To Tom's surprise, Tall Oak handed him a tomahawk. He gave Zuma a spear.

"You both proved yourselves today on the river," the chief said in his deep voice. "I would be honoured if you would fight with us to save my daughter." Then he turned to Rising Sun and gave him a bow and a quiver. "Son, this was my own father's bow. Use it bravely. Will you ask the spirits to bless us in our task?"

"Yes, Father," Rising Sun said solemnly. He chanted a few words and Tall Oak nodded his approval.

As they trudged through the storm, the snow flew in their faces, nearly blinding them. Tom heard a panicked yelp and turned to see that Chilli had fallen into a snowdrift.

"Quick!" cried Zuma. "Get him out!"

It took several minutes to dig the little dog out of the deep snow. When they finally pulled him free, the Chihuahua was shivering.

"He only has short fur," Zuma said, rubbing him all over. "He and I just aren't made for this cold."

The war party fought their way through

the snow until they reached the Mohawk village. Gliding Eagle, who was leading the way, stopped dead in his tracks. The other braves shook their heads. Chief Tall Oak looked utterly defeated.

"What's wrong?" asked Zuma. "What's the problem?"

"The problem," said Rising Sun, "is that they've palisaded their village." He pointed to the tall wooden fence that encircled the Mohawk settlement. It was made from tree trunks sharpened into dangerous-looking points. Tom guessed it had been built recently, as the wood still looked and smelled fresh. It had certainly taken the Mohicans by surprise.

"Palisaded?" Zuma repeated. "What does that mean?"

"It means," said Tom, "that we can't get in."

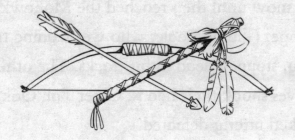

CHAPTER 7
SNOWED IN

"We can burn it down!"

Tom turned to see who had spoken, and saw that Waning Moon was already reaching into a beaded pouch on his belt for a flint.

"No!" said Tall Oak firmly, holding up one hand. "No fire."

"Why not?"

"Because Laughing Brook is somewhere inside that fence," said Rising Sun. "And we don't want her to be hurt."

Waning Moon turned away, ashamed he hadn't realised that himself.

"Let's just force our way through the entrance," suggested Gliding Eagle. "There has to be a gap to let people in and out."

The chief frowned. "The entrance will be guarded, and we'll lose the element of surprise."

The chief and the older braves argued, trying to decide the best way to get into the enemy village. As he tried to think of a plan, Tom picked up a handful of snow and absent-mindedly began shaping it into a sphere.

"What are you doing?" Zuma asked.

"Making a snowball," Tom replied. "My friends and I do this at home when it snows. Then we throw them at each other."

"That sounds fun," said Zuma.

Tom laughed. "It is! We call them snowball fights."

"What else do you do with snow?" Zuma asked.

"Lots of cool things. We build snowmen, and go sledging down hills. Sometimes, when the snow is deep enough, we even build forts by piling up snow really high and—" Tom stopped talking and grinned. He'd suddenly had a brilliant idea.

"I know how we're going to get into that village!" he called over to the braves.

The warriors looked at Tom, clearly doubtful that a boy could have the solution, but they stopped talking and listened to what he had to say.

"All we have to do is pile as much snow as we can right up against that fence. If we pack it tightly and make a slope, we can climb up and jump over the fence. The snow on the other side will break our fall so we won't get hurt."

"How clever!" said Zuma.

The braves agreed and wasted no time getting started. Working quickly, they scooped up armfuls of snow. Luckily, the howling wind drowned out the noise they were making, so the Mohawk couldn't hear them. Before long, there was a small mountain of snow beside the fence. Next, they shaped the snow into a strong ramp, leading right up to the top of the palisade.

That would be so fun to slide down, Tom thought wistfully. But this was no time for playing – they had to save Laughing Brook.

Rising Sun stepped forward.

"When we hit the ground on the other

side, we'll split up and start searching for Laughing Brook," he said. "Tom, Zuma and I will search the longhouses. Gliding Eagle, you and Waning Moon get ready to attack; everyone else split up and look for her in the wigwams."

As Rising Sun rattled off his orders, Tom glanced over at Tall Oak. The chief looked proud of the way his son was taking charge.

"We will catch the Mohawk warriors unawares, but their surprise won't last long," Rising Sun finished. "Thanks to Tom, getting in will be easy enough. But we will still have to fight our way out."

Tom, Zuma and Rising Sun climbed the snow ramp first. The soles of their leather moccasins slipped on the icy

surface, but after a few false attempts they
made it to the top. Tom looked down at the
Mohawk village.

It had wigwams and longhouses, just like the Mohican village. Hoping there wasn't a Mohawk guard waiting below, he jumped over the fence and landed in the soft snow.

Zuma jumped straight after him, still holding Chilli, and Rising Sun followed. They could hear the other braves scrambling up the slope, but they didn't wait for them. Moving as quietly as they could, they trudged through the snow towards the nearest longhouse.

"This must be the Mohawk chief's house," explained Rising Sun. "It's the biggest one in the village."

Gathering their courage, they crept inside. Several generations of Mohawk tribesmen, women and children slept soundly on raised platforms, covered with thick furs and heavy blankets. A small fire burned in the centre of

the longhouse, giving them just enough light
to see.

Zuma set Chilli down on the ground and
whispered, "Help us find Laughing Brook,
boy."

They tiptoed through the longhouse with
Chilli in the lead, sniffing frantically. As he
searched for Rising Sun's sister, Tom noticed
something sparkling in the dim light. He
crept closer to investigate. The light was
shining from a belt made of
woven rope and seashells
that hung from a peg on
the wall. And right in the
middle was a gold disc with
a sun stamped on it – the
Aztec coin!

He grabbed Zuma's hand
and pointed. Her eyes lit up

and she began moving towards the golden disc.

But just then Chilli gave a little yelp of delight. He scampered over to a sleeping figure huddled beneath a bearskin.

"Laughing Brook!" Rising Sun whispered.

Chilli began to lick Laughing Brook's palm, hoping for another deer jerky treat. The Mohican girl sat up and rubbed her eyes, looking confused and afraid. But when she spotted her brother, a smile of joy spread across her face.

"Did you three come alone?" she whispered in disbelief.

"The others are outside," Rising Sun told her. "We must hurry!"

Laughing Brook got up quietly and they started tiptoeing towards the exit.

"Wait," whispered Zuma. "We can't go

without the coin!"

Tom's heart raced as Zuma went back to where they'd spied the belt. When she was halfway there, a loud grunt sounded through the longhouse. Tom froze in terror and Rising Sun raised his tomahawk. But the grunt was followed by a loud snore, as a Mohawk brave turned over in his sleep.

Tom let out a sigh of relief. Only Chilli was unaware of what danger they were in. He wagged his tail excitedly, hoping that Laughing Brook would give him a deer jerky treat.

Zuma tiptoed closer to the belt. When she was nearly close enough to take it, Chilli's wagging tail collided with a clay pot. The pot fell on its side and smashed, spilling beads everywhere.

Tom stifled a groan.

"Uh-oh!" said Zuma, freezing again.

The sound of the crashing pottery woke up the entire longhouse. Babies cried out and grown-ups yawned and stretched as they sat up and peered around in the dim light.

A large man leaped from his sleeping platform, instantly alert. From the way everyone turned to him for guidance, Tom guessed he was the Mohawk chief. The man grabbed a tomahawk and pointed it at the intruders.

"Mohican invaders!" he shouted. "Capture them!"

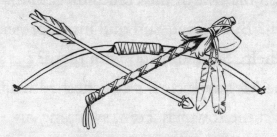

CHAPTER 8
TOMAHAWK TERROR

The Mohawk chief let out a war cry and charged towards them. The other Mohawk braves jumped from their beds, grabbed their weapons and joined the attack.

"Run!" cried Zuma, scooping Chilli into her arms and heading for the door.

Laughing Brook and Rising Sun were right behind Zuma, but Tom couldn't move. If they left the coin behind, he and Zuma might be stuck here forever. Should he try to grab the belt in the confusion and run off with it? But Rising Sun and his sister needed their help. Should he go with them?

The Mohawk chief's eyes flashed wildly as he came towards Tom, swinging his tomahawk. It was too late to run. Now Tom had no choice but to try and defend himself.

He raised his own tomahawk and braced himself for an attack.

The Mohawk chief was almost upon him, but instead of feeling the impact of a blade, Tom heard a slipping noise, followed by a gasp. In the next heartbeat, he felt the whistling breeze of something flying just over his head. It was followed by a loud *thwummmppp*.

Tom opened his eyes to see the mighty Mohawk leader sprawled on his back on the dirt floor in a sea of brightly coloured beads. His tomahawk had flown through the air and lodged itself in the far wall of the longhouse.

Tom took off like a shot, following his friends out of the longhouse.

By now the whole Mohawk tribe was awake. A ferocious battle was in full force.

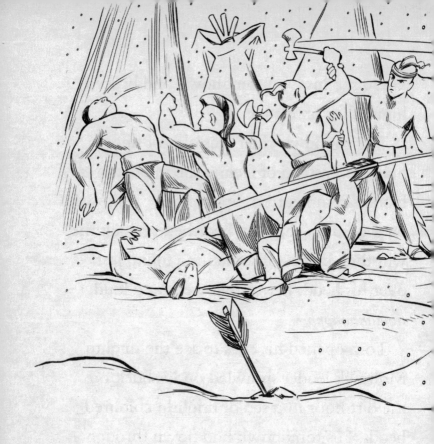

"We've got to get Laughing Brook out of here," said Rising Sun.

"Let's keep to the shadows," said Tom. "If we stay close to the fence, we might make it to the entrance without being noticed."

They pressed themselves against the
tall wooden posts and pushed through the
snow as quickly as they could. All around
them spears flew and arrows sailed past
like missiles. Even the howling of the wind

couldn't drown out the warriors' cries as they flung their tomahawks around.

Although the Mohican were outnumbered, the element of surprise had helped them. Already, several Mohawk lay wounded in the snow. Tom saw Tall Oak and Gliding Eagle right in the middle of the fighting. Standing back to back, they fired off arrow after arrow, hitting an enemy target every time.

"Hurry," Laughing Brook urged them. "The entrance isn't far away."

Tom felt a surge of relief, knowing they were so close to safety. Only a few more steps and they'd be—

"Where do you think you're going?"

A towering Mohawk warrior stepped into their path. His face was splattered with blood and despite the cold his broad chest was bare, revealing scars from former battles. He glowered down at them.

"Er… nowhere," said Zuma. "We were just leaving."

The warrior laughed, but it was a humourless sound. "Nobody leaves unless I say so."

"This is Wildfire," Laughing Brook explained. "He's the Mohawk chief's eldest son."

"At least let my sister and the two children go," insisted Rising Sun. "You can fight me instead."

"Well, this is a stroke of luck," Wildfire said with a wicked grin. "Not only do we have the chief's pretty daughter, now we also have his son! What better way to convince Tall Oak to turn over the hunting grounds and fishing weirs to the Mohawk tribe than by holding *both* his children captive!"

"My father would never do that!" said Rising Sun, standing tall and raising his weapon.

"He might," said Wildfire, "if I threaten to scalp you! Which is exactly what I *will* do if you take one more step."

Zuma gasped. Chilli whimpered. Rising Sun bravely positioned himself like a human shield in front of his sister. But Tom had an idea.

He quickly reached down, scooped up a handful of snow and packed it into a hard sphere. Then he flung the icy ball at Wildfire, hitting him right between the eyes.

While the Mohawk was wiping away the snow, Rising Sun yelled and charged at him with all his might. The Mohawk warrior fell backwards, the wind knocked out of him.

"He won't be down for long," said Laughing Brook. "Let's get out of here!"

"You go," said Rising Sun. "I'll stay and fight."

"So will I!" said Tom.

"Me too," said Zuma, thrusting a squirming Chilli into Laughing Brook's arms.

But before the three of them could enter the battle, Laughing Brook gasped and pointed.

"Look, there's Waning Moon," she said. "He's in trouble!"

Moonlight reflecting off the white snow had lit up a terrible sight. A Mohawk brave had shoved Waning Moon against the wooden fence, and was holding a tomahawk to his throat.

"We have to help him!" said Tom.

"How?" asked Rising Sun, shaking his head. "We'll never get there in time!"

"We don't have to," said Zuma, lifting her spear.

She bent back her arm, took aim and hurled the weapon with all her might. It streaked through

the air, heading right for Waning Moon's
attacker. The tip of the spear caught the
Mohawk by his buckskin shirt,
pinning his sleeve to the
fence. He dropped his
tomahawk in surprise
and Waning Moon
wriggled free.
"That was brilliant!"
said Tom.

But his relief didn't last long. Because
Wildfire had regained consciousness. He
grabbed Laughing Brook's ankle, dragging
her down into the snow. Then he scrambled
to his feet and stood above her, a murderous
look in his eyes.

"Help!" cried Laughing Brook.

"Leave my sister alone!" demanded Rising
Sun.

But Wildfire drew a knife from his belt.

"The son of a Mohawk chief will not be defeated by *children*," he spat out. "If any of you so much as moves, the squaw dies."

Wildfire jerked Laughing Brook to her feet and began pulling her towards a wigwam. She fought and kicked, but she was no match for the strong brave.

Tom knew it would take a lot more than a snowball to stop him this time. He thought about throwing his tomahawk at Wildfire, but the risk of hitting Laughing Brook was too high. Rising Sun's aim was even worse than his, and Zuma had already thrown her spear. Tom had never felt so helpless.

The chief's daughter was far more valuable to the Mohawk alive than dead, but there was something in Wildfire's war-crazed eyes that made Tom think the warrior might scalp poor Laughing Brook just for fun. It wasn't just about tribal rivalries now, it was about family honour. In the time he'd spent with the Mohicans, Tom had seen how much family meant to the Native Americans. Suddenly he had an idea.

He cupped his hands to his mouth and shouted at the top of his lungs. "Chief Tall Oak! Laughing Brook needs your help!"

Even over the din of the battle, the Mohican chief heard Tom calling out the name of his cherished daughter. He spun in their direction, his arrow poised and his bowstring pulled taut. When he saw Laughing Brook being dragged off by the Mohawk warrior, he let out a cry of rage.

The chief let the arrow fly. Even though he was firing from a distance, the arrow lodged in Wildfire's leg.

Howling in pain, Wildfire let go of Laughing Brook and grabbed his calf. Red blood poured out of his wound on to the white snow.

"Aaaaarrrrghhhh!" the Mohawk warrior screamed. The sound of his cry was so chilling that all the warriors stopped fighting.

"Finish him off, Rising Sun!" shouted Chief Tall Oak.

Rising Sun moved slowly towards the fallen Mohawk brave, tomahawk in hand. An eerie silence fell over the settlement as Rising Sun reached his enemy and raised his weapon. But instead of swinging it at Wildfire, he dropped the tomahawk down into the snow. He closed his eyes and began to chant. His words were barely a whisper, but they seemed to fill the air like the swirling snowflakes. Then he bent down

and carefully removed the arrow from the
Mohawk warrior's leg.

Wildfire let out a sharp gasp, but his
screams stopped. Everyone watched as
Rising Sun took off his headband and
wrapped it tightly round the warrior's
wounded calf.

"Why is he doing that?" Zuma whispered.

"He's using it to stop the bleeding," Tom
replied.

"No, I mean why is he helping the enemy?" Zuma sounded shocked. "Wildfire threatened to scalp Laughing Brook."

"All life is precious," said Rising Sun, answering Zuma's question. "Even that of my enemy. If I do not stop the bleeding, he will die."

Wildfire lay shivering in the snow. He no longer looked like a terrifying warrior. Now he just looked scared. Zuma removed her fur cloak and gently laid it over the wounded man like a blanket. Tom offered his own cloak as a pillow.

Everyone watched silently as Rising Sun continued his chant, asking the spirits to help Wildfire.

Suddenly a shadow fell over them.

Tom looked up and saw the Mohawk chief looming above them.

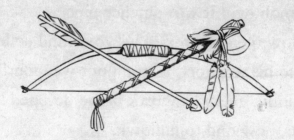

CHAPTER 9
SWEATING IT OUT

Tom looked straight into the eyes of the
Mohawk chief. The enormous man was
holding an object high above his head.
Thinking it was the tomahawk that had
narrowly missed his head back in the
longhouse, Tom raised his own tomahawk
and dropped into a defensive crouch.

"It's OK, Tom," said Zuma. "I think he
wants to be friends."

The mighty Mohawk chief wasn't holding

a tomahawk. It was a peace pipe.

Now the chief raised his voice and called out to his warriors, "Drop your weapons!" Instantly, every Mohawk brave dropped his spear, bow and tomahawk.

"The Mohawk tribe surrenders," said the chief, in a deep, steady voice. "We wish to make peace."

Chief Tall Oak walked over to the Mohawk chief. "We would like that." He ordered his own braves to drop their weapons, and all of them quickly obeyed.

"What made you change your mind?" asked Zuma.

The chief's eyes settled on Rising Sun, who was still tending to Wildfire's wound. "This young brave has helped my son. He asked the sacred spirits to ease my boy's pain. He has taught me an important lesson

– there is no greater power than kindness."

Chief Tall Oak looked at his own son with obvious pride on his face.

Maybe he has learned that healers can be as powerful as warriors, thought Tom.

By now the Mohawk medicine man had joined Rising Sun. Together they spread a salve on Wildfire's wound and chanted. The bleeding had stopped and he was no longer writhing in pain.

"I was wrong to wage war on my neighbours," the chief said to Tall Oak. "The price of violence is much too high. Now I know how you must have suffered when we took your daughter. If I had lost my son, the pain would be too great to bear."

"From this day forward, we will live in peace," said Tall Oak. "We will share the vast forest and the deep waters, and all the bounty they provide."

"And we will be grateful," added Tall Oak, "for all that we have, and the beauty and goodness that the spirits have bestowed upon us."

Rising Sun called over a group of Mohawk braves and instructed them to carry

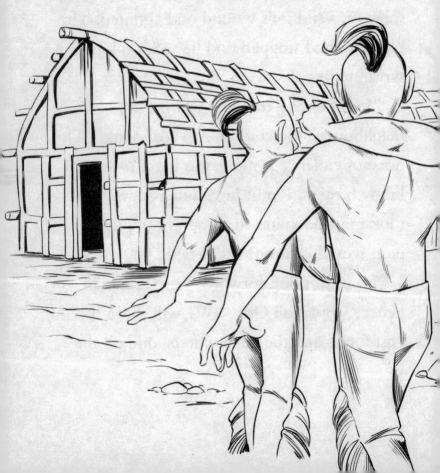

Wildfire back to his longhouse to rest.

"The storm still rages, and it would be unwise to venture back across the river now," said the Mohawk chief. "You can warm yourselves here until it's over."

That sounded like a great idea to Tom. He was cold and exhausted from the long night of fighting. And they still had to get the gold coin!

"Quick," he whispered to Zuma. "Let's go back to the chief's longhouse." But before they could sneak away, the Mohawk chief made an announcement.

"Together we will all purify our battle-weary bodies and souls," he said. He turned to his medicine man. "Clever Fox, go now and prepare the sweat lodge."

"Sweat lodge?" said Tom. "That sounds… smelly."

"We Aztecs have sweat houses too," said Zuma. "Water is poured over hot stones to make steam. The heat makes you sweat and leaves you feeling warm, clean and very relaxed."

"I suppose it *will* be nice to get out of this cold," said Tom. But he didn't have a choice. The Mohawk chief was guiding everyone who had fought towards the sweat lodge.

The next thing Tom knew, he, Zuma and the others were sitting on tree trunks in a steamy room. The warriors prayed and sang to their gods, as sweat dripped down their bodies. Even though the warmth felt nice, Tom couldn't relax. He knew they had to get that gold coin!

"Zuma," he whispered, "let's see if we can sneak out now."

The Aztec girl nodded, but as they got up, so did the other warriors. They began to file out of the sweat lodge. Outside, Tom was surprised to see that the snow had stopped falling and the air had lost some of its chill. A layer of fresh snow covered the village, erasing all trace of the bloody battle.

The Mohawk braves lit an enormous fire. Everyone gathered round, dancing and drumming, celebrating their new friendship. As the two tribes danced, Tom quietly slipped away from the crowd and headed towards the chief's longhouse. But suddenly

a large hand clapped him on the shoulder
and pulled him back.

"Where are you going?" boomed Chief
Tall Oak. "You helped bring peace to our

people. You must celebrate with us!"

Tom didn't dare argue. He returned to the party and joined in the dancing. As the sun rose in the dawn sky, the two chiefs brought the celebration to an end.

Gliding Eagle, Waning Moon and the other Mohican warriors went ahead to clear a path through the snow from the village to the river. Tall Oak, the children and Chilli stayed behind to say goodbye to the Mohawk chief.

"Before we part, I wish to give a gift of thanks," said the Mohawk chief, "to my neighbour and friend." He handed Tall Oak an item made of rope and shells. "This is a storytelling belt. It recounts the myth of Sky Woman, and how she created the world." His face lit with a smile. "A world made for all to share."

In the pale glow of the sunrise, something at the centre of the belt caught the light, throwing off bright rays of gold.

"It's the belt with the coin in it!" Tom whispered to Zuma.

Tall Oak took the beautiful belt and turned to Rising Sun. "This gift is precious," he said in a solemn voice. "It represents goodness, wisdom and honour."

"Yes," said Rising Sun, "it is fitting that you should have it, Father."

Chief Tall Oak shook his head. "It is even more fitting that *you* should have it." He smiled and handed the belt to his son. "I am proud of you, Rising Sun. You are good, and wise, and honourable."

Rising Sun smiled as he took the belt. "Thank you, Father. But I couldn't have done it without my friends." He turned to Tom and

Zuma. "You two showed me that you don't have to be a mighty warrior to be brave." He held out the belt to Tom and Zuma.

"That's really kind of you, Rising Sun," said Zuma. "But we don't need the whole belt."

"You deserve it more than us," said Tom. "But maybe we could just have that shiny round thing in the centre, as a memento?"

Gliding Eagle took an arrow from his

quiver and helped Rising Sun remove the Aztec coin from the belt. Then Rising Sun handed it to Zuma.

As soon as the gold coin was in Zuma's grasp, a magical mist began to swirl around her. Tom picked up Chilli and took Zuma's hand. The mist grew thicker and spun faster around them.

"Goodbye, Rising Sun!" called Tom. "You're going to be a great medicine man!"

"I will call on the spirits to guide you home safely, my friends," Rising Sun shouted back over the wind.

And as the mist lifted them up, Tom caught one last look at the Mohawk village, sparkling under a layer of white snow, before they began their journey through time and space.

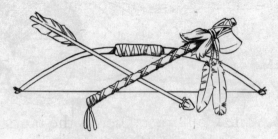

CHAPTER 10
TRICK OR TREAT

They landed safely in Tom's garden, only moments after they'd left. Tom's mother was still in the potting shed, searching for a bag for the leaves.

Zuma, back in her blue paint and feathers, stood up in the middle of the vegetable patch. She brushed off the soil from her bottom and said, "At least it was a soft landing."

Tom looked round and saw the mess that

Tlaloc had made stomping about with his enormous feet. "We'd better clean this up quickly!"

Zuma and Tom raked the leaves back into a pile, while Chilli raced across the garden chasing squirrels.

"It's nice to be away from all that snow and horrible weather," Zuma said, lifting her face to the sun.

Suddenly, a rumble of thunder sounded.

"Spoke too soon," groaned Tom.

Once again, Tlaloc appeared before them. His blue skin was even brighter than the cloudless sky.

"Got it!" Zuma said, holding up the coin with a cheeky grin.

The rain god scowled and snatched the sun coin out of her hand.

"Only one more to go," said Tom.

"That may be so. But your final quest will be the most difficult yet." Tlaloc sneered, showing his fangs. "There may be only one more coin," Tlaloc reminded them in his rumbling voice, "but don't expect to find it. EVER!" Then he stomped his feet and vanished in another crash of thunder.

"Do you think he means that?" Zuma asked, biting her lip.

"I'm afraid so," said Tom. "Although it's hard to imagine what could be worse than warring Native American tribes and a blizzard…"

"I can think of one thing that would be much worse," said Zuma. "Not finding the last coin and never being free."

They were quiet for a moment, wondering what Tlaloc had in store for them next. What would Zuma do if they failed?

No, Tom thought. *We won't fail. I won't let that happen. I'll do everything I possibly can to help Zuma win her freedom.*

"Whatever Tlaloc sends our way, we can handle it if we stick together," Tom said. "One more adventure, and then you'll be free." He grinned. "But in the meantime, let's do something fun!"

"Like what?" asked Zuma.

"Like getting ready for Halloween!" cried Tom. "We can start right now, by carving our jack-o'-lantern."

He ran across the garden to the vegetable patch and chose the biggest, most orange pumpkin he could find. Then Tom and Zuma went inside the house.

"Dad!" Tom called.

Dr Sullivan wandered into the kitchen, holding a thick book called *The Native Peoples of North America*. On the cover was a picture of a stern Mohican who looked a lot like Chief Tall Oak.

"Can you help me carve a jack-o'-lantern?" Tom asked.

Dad put down his book and got a knife from the kitchen drawer. He carefully cut a circle out of the top of the pumpkin and removed it by the stem. Then Tom and Zuma reached inside and pulled out the slimy seeds.

"I used to have to do this all the time when I was a slave," Zuma said, wrinkling her nose. "I guess pumpkins are still as fiddly as they were hundreds of years ago!"

"Did you know that the Native Americans used to eat pumpkins?" Tom's dad asked him.

"I did, actually," said Tom, grinning at Zuma, as Dad set to work carving out eyes, nose and a mouth.

Mum came in just as they were finishing.

"My goodness!" she cried. "That's terrifying."

She fished around in a kitchen drawer and pulled out a candle. Lighting it carefully, she passed it to Tom, who placed it inside the jack-o'-lantern.

"There," he said. "All done! Let's put it on the front steps," Tom cried, as he and Zuma took the glowing pumpkin outdoors. "That will really scare the trick-or-treaters."

They put it on the front porch and smiled proudly at their handiwork.

"That's the thing about these adventures," he said. "No matter what tricks Tlaloc has planned for us, some parts of time travelling are a real treat!"

TIME HUNTERS

TURN THE PAGE TO . . .

➤ Meet the REAL Mohican Braves!

➤ Find out fantastic FACTS!

➤ Battle with your GAMING CARDS!

➤ And MUCH MORE!

WHO WERE THE MIGHTIEST MOHICAN BRAVES?

Crazy Horse was a *real* Brave. Find out more about him and other famous Braves!

CRAZY HORSE was a Native American war leader who fought to keep the Lakota tribe's traditional ways. He had a vision when he was young that told him that he would protect his people. He even saw the lightning bolt that he would wear as face paint in battle! When the Lakota people were ordered to move on to reservations, Crazy Horse refused. In June 1876, Crazy Horse bravely led 1,500 Sioux warriors to victory against the US cavalry at the Battle of the Little Bighorn.

MOHICAN
CRAZY HORSE

Brain Power	
Fear Factor	250
Bravery	320
Weapon: Tomahawk	330
	315

— TOTAL 1215 —

GERONIMO was born in 1829 in what is now New Mexico. When Mexican soldiers raided his camp and murdered his family, Geronimo vowed to get revenge. For the next ten years, Geronimo and a small band of Apache warriors attacked Mexican towns.

MOHICAN

GERONIMO

Brain Power	280
Fear Factor	250
Bravery	300
Weapon: Rifle	320

— TOTAL 1150 —

When the United States took over Mexican land in 1848 and pushed the Apache people on to reservations, Geronimo and his followers fought them, attacking American troops across the American Southwest. For years he famously avoided being captured, but in 1886 he surrendered. In later life he became a celebrity, attending fairs, publishing his autobiography and even getting to meet the president.

SITTING BULL — one of the most famous and powerful Native American chiefs — was born around 1831 in the Dakota Territories. A skilled hunter, he killed his first buffalo aged only ten. At a Sun Dance Ceremony in 1876, Sitting Bull danced for 36 hours straight! He fought alongside Crazy Horse at the Battle of the Little Bighorn, defeating General Custer and his men. After the battle, Sitting Bull fled to Canada. Years later, he returned to the US and joined Buffalo Bill Cody's Wild West show. While performing in the show he became friends with the sharpshooter, Annie Oakley, and eventually adopted her as his daughter.

MOHICAN
SITTING BULL

Brain Power	
Fear Factor	300
Bravery	265
Weapon: Spear	295
	260
TOTAL 1120	

SHABASH was a Mohican chief who lived in what is now New York. He had a very hard start in life. When he was only four years old, his mother was killed by Mohawk warriors, then he lost his sister and brother to smallpox.

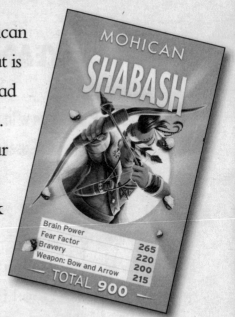

MOHICAN
SHABASH

Brain Power	265
Fear Factor	220
Bravery	200
Weapon: Bow and Arrow	215
TOTAL	900

Shabash sold his family's lands to the government and began drinking heavily. However, a vision told him he must find a way to help his people and to please God. Shabash converted to Christianity, and became a respected leader, who worked hard to protect his people from exploitation.

WEAPONS

Crazy Horse was a demon with a tomahawk! Find out what other weapons were used by Native Americans.

Bow and Arrow: The most common weapon used by Native Americans. Good for long range, and accuracy.

Tomahawk: An axe-like weapon with a wooden handle. It could be used in close-contact fighting, or it could be thrown.

Spear: Used both for hunting, and in battle. They could be long or short.

Rifle: After the European settlers came, the Native Americans acquired their weapons, most famously – the Winchester rifle, used in the victory against General Custer in The Battle of the Little Bighorn.

MOHICAN BRAVE TIMELINE

In MOHICAN BRAVE Tom and Zuma meet some NATIVE AMERICANS. Discover more about it in this brilliant timeline!

AD 1492
Christopher Columbus lands in North America.

AD 1675–1676
Native Americans fight against British settlers in King Philip's War.

AD 1815–1817
Escaped slaves and Native Americans fight against the US in the First Seminole War.

AD 1607
British settlers arrive at Jamestown, Virginia.

AD 1763
King George III stops English settlement west of the Appalachian mountains to ease tensions with the Native Americans.

AD 1835–1843
The Second Seminole War starts.

AD 1876 The US army is defeated by Native Americans at the Battle of the Little Bighorn.

AD 1830
The Indian Removal Act forces Native Americans to move west.

AD 1862
The Homestead Act allows settlers to move on to Native American land.

AD 1924
Native Americans are declared US citizens.

TIME HUNTERS TIMELINE

Tom and Zuma never know where in history they'll travel to next!
Check out in what order their adventures actually happen.

10,000 BC–3000 BC
The Stone Age

AD 1427–AD 1521
The Aztec Empire

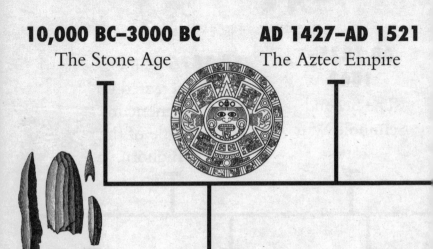

AD 1185–AD 1868
Feudal Japan

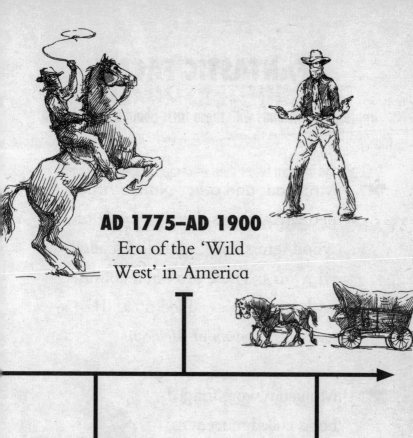

AD 1775–AD 1900
Era of the 'Wild
West' in America

AD 1492–AD 1607
First contact between
Native American
tribes and European
settlers in America

AD 1850–AD 1880
Bushranger outlaws
become famous
in Australia

FANTASTIC FACTS

Impress your friends with these facts about the Wild West.

➤ Mohicans and other Native American people lived in structures made of wood, grass, bark and cloth called wigwams. These are often confused with tent houses called tipis. *'We-ku-wuhm' is wigwam in Mohican!*

➤ Mohicans wore fringed boots called moccasins, breechcloths and leggings. Men and women often wore their hair in two long braids and wore feathers in their hair on special occasions. *I might try that.*

The 'Mohawk' hairstyle was worn by tribesmen hoping to intimidate their enemies in battle. Instead of shaving the sides of their heads, they would pull out hair in clumps. *Ouch!*

The Mohican tribe were famous for their beautiful beadwork. They crafted 'wampum' beads out of white and purple shells, often weaving them into belts given as gifts or used as money. *That's some belt!*

Native Americans used canoes made by digging out and shaping trees. They were used when fishing or travelling by water. *Almost as fun as a lilo!*

WHO IS THE MIGHTIEST?

Collect the Gaming Cards and play!

Battle with a friend to find out which historical hero is the mightiest of them all!

Players: 2
Number of Cards: 4+ each

→ Players start with an equal number of cards. Decide which player goes first.

→ Player 1: choose a category from your first card (Brain Power, Fear Factor, Bravery or Weapon), and read out the score.

→ Player 2: read out the stat from the same category on your first card.

➤ The player with the highest score wins the round, takes their opponent's card and puts it at the back of their own pack.

➤ The winning player then chooses a category from the next card and play continues.

➤ The game continues until one player has won all the cards. The last card played wins the title 'Mightiest hero of them all!'

COWBOYS
WYATT EARP

Brain Power	300
Fear Factor	285
Bravery	320
Weapon: Bullwhip	330
TOTAL	1235

For more fantastic games go to:
www.time–hunters.com

BATTLE THE MIGHTIEST!

Collect a new set of mighty warriors — free in every Time Hunters book! Have you got them all?

COWBOYS

- [ ] Wyatt Earp
- [ ] Wild Bill Hickok
- [ ] Buffalo Bill
- [ ] Billy the Kid

SAMURAI

- [ ] Lord Kenshin
- [ ] Honda Tadakatsu
- [ ] Lord Shingen
- [ ] Hattori Hanzo

OUTBACK OUTLAWS

- [ ] Ben Hall
- [ ] Captain Thunderbolt
- [ ] Frank Gardiner
- [ ] Ned Kelly

STONE AGE MEN

- ☐ Gam
- ☐ Col
- ☐ Orm
- ☐ Pag

BRAVES

- ☐ Shabash
- ☐ Crazy Horse
- ☐ Geronimo
- ☐ Sitting Bull

AZTECS

- ☐ Ahuizotl
- ☐ Zuma
- ☐ Tlaloc
- ☐ Moctezuma II

STONE AGE

GAM

Brain Power	
Fear Factor	280
Bravery	300
Weapon: Stone Axe	345
	320

TOTAL 1245

MOHICAN

SHABASH

Brain Power	
Fear Factor	265
Bravery	220
Weapon: Bow and Arrow	200
	215

TOTAL 900

AZTEC

AHUIZOTL

Brain Power	
Fear Factor	280
Bravery	250
Weapon: Macuahuitl	250
	280

TOTAL 1060

MORE MIGHTY WARRIORS!

Don't forget to collect these warriors from Tom's
first adventure!

GLADIATORS

- [ ] Hilarus
- [ ] Spartacus
- [ ] Flamma
- [ ] Emperor Commodus

KNIGHTS

- [ ] King Arthur
- [ ] Galahad
- [ ] Lancelot
- [ ] Gawain

VIKINGS

- [ ] Erik the Red
- [ ] Harald Bluetooth
- [ ] Ivar the Boneless
- [ ] Canute the Great

GREEKS

- [ ] Hector
- [ ] Ajax
- [ ] Achilles
- [ ] Odysseus

PIRATES

- [ ] Blackbeard
- [ ] Captain Kidd
- [ ] Henry Morgan
- [ ] Calico Jack

EGYPTIANS

- [ ] Anubis
- [ ] King Tut
- [ ] Isis
- [ ] Tom

Who were the Aztecs?
How did they live?
What weapons did they fight with?

Join Tom and Zuma on another action-packed Time Hunters adventure!

As they travelled back through time, Tom could feel his heart thumping in his chest. They had already gone to some very dangerous places, from the Wild West to the harsh Australian outback, but what was in store for them now? The god was cruel enough to send them anywhere – to the inside of a volcano, or the bottom of the ocean!

So he was relieved when the sparkling mist faded and he felt solid ground beneath his feet. Tom looked around quickly, and gasped. It looked like some kind of paradise. All around were tall trees and thick bushes of emerald green. Flowers blazed in every colour of the rainbow. A waterfall poured over rocks into a crystal-clear pool.

Tom wiped his forehead. Wherever they were, it was hot. He was already sweating.

Zuma squealed with delight. "My old clothes!" she said happily. "The jungle! I'm home!"

Tom turned to see Zuma dancing for joy. Chilli was scampering happily around her feet. The slave girl's headdress and blue paint had disappeared. Now she was wearing a loose white blouse with short sleeves and a white skirt, both with bright red bands sewn along the bottom. Her dark hair was loose and shining. Only the gleaming black pendant she always wore round her neck remained.

Zuma stopped dancing and looked at Tom. "Nice clothes," she giggled.

Looking down, Tom saw that his football kit was gone. Instead he was dressed in a blue cloak, with a white cloth wrapped round his waist like a short skirt. "Thanks," he said, blushing. He pulled the cloak round himself to hide his bare chest and legs.

"You'll get used to it," Zuma smiled. "It's too hot here in Mexico to wear lots of clothes."

Tom would have preferred a T-shirt and shorts, but Zuma was right – it was hot and steamy, even beneath the shady trees. "So we're back in Aztec times?" he said, looking around. "Cool!"

"Wait until you see one of our cities," Zuma replied. A dreamy look crossed her face. "There are pyramids shining beneath the sun, great squares…"

"…and human sacrifices," Tom reminded her. "It may be your home, but don't forget how dangerous it is. Tlaloc said it would be our toughest challenge yet." He pointed at the black stone hanging round Zuma's neck. "Let's ask your necklace for help."

Zuma's pendant was magical and gave them clues to where Tlaloc had hidden the coins. "OK," she sighed. "But it will only be another silly riddle."

Tom grinned. Unlike the Aztec girl, he enjoyed trying to work out the pendant's clues. He watched with excitement as Zuma held up the black disc and began chanting softly:

"Mirror, mirror, on a chain,
Can you help us? Please explain!
We are lost and must be told
How to find the coins of gold."

Tom and Zuma leaned over the pendant as ghostly white words appeared on the stone:

Find the city on the eagle's path;
Use the stream to escape a god's wrath.
Beware the man who bears a disguise;
A false face hides the ultimate prize.
When fur and feathers fight for control,
The ring of stone is your ultimate goal.

Climb up to the house of rain;
The flying spear will end your pain.

As the words faded away, Tom saw that Zuma had gone pale. "What's wrong?" he asked.

"For once I understand some of this," she replied softly. "I think the house of rain means Tlaloc's temple in the Aztec capital, Tenochtitlan. That's where I was nearly sacrificed."

During their adventures together, Zuma had proved her bravery time and time again. This was the first time Tom had seen her look nervous. Then again, it wasn't that surprising. The last time she had visited Tlaloc's temple, the slave girl had only just escaped with her life.

"Don't worry," Tom said. "I'll be with you this time."

Zuma smiled as Chilli jumped up, putting his front paws on her knee. "I know, little doggie, you'll be there too." She grinned at the Chihuahua. "And we got out together last time, didn't we?"

"The sooner we find Tlaloc's coin, the sooner you won't have to worry any more," Tom said firmly. "So let's get started. The riddle said we have to find the city on the eagle's path. Any idea what that means?"

Zuma shrugged and said, "I got the bit about the house of rain, but the rest is gibberish to me. Anyway, you're the brainbox. I don't see why I should have to solve it all—"

The slave girl froze. Following her gaze, Tom saw that a nearby bush was rustling. He crouched down and peered through the leaves. A furry, cat-like creature was hiding in the undergrowth!

Tom gulped. He had read about the dangerous animals you might meet in the jungle. Without weapons, he and Zuma wouldn't stand a chance. As the bush rustled again and the creature emerged, he realised there was no time to run…

"Oh no," hissed Zuma. "It's a jaguar!"

They were going to be a big cat's dinner!

THE HUNT CONTINUES...

Travel through time with Tom and Zuma as they battle the mightiest warriors of the past. Will they find all six coins and win Zuma's freedom? Find out in:

Got it! ☐

Got it! ☐

Got it! ☐

Got it!

☐

Got it!

☐

Got it!

☐

Tick off the books as you collect them!

DISCOVER A NEW TIME HUNTERS QUEST!

Tom's first adventure was with an Ancient Egyptian mummy called Isis. Can Tom and Isis track down the six hidden amulets scattered through history? Find out in:

Got it!

Got it!

Got it!

Got it! ☐

Got it! ☐

Got it! ☐

Tick off the books as you collect them!

Go to:

www.time-hunters.com

Travel through time and join the hunt for the
mightiest heroes and villains of history to win
brilliant prizes!

For more adventures, awesome card
games, competitions and thrilling news,
scan this QR code*: